The Berenstain Bears' Really BIG PET SHOW

We love our pets,
We love them so
that all our pets
are "Best in Show."

BIG PET SHOW

Jan & Mike Berenstain

HarperFestival®
A Division of HarperCollinsPublishers
The Berenstain Bears' Really Big Pet Show
Copyright © 2008 by Berenstain Bears, Inc.
HarperCollins®, ■®, and HarperFestival® are trademarks of HarperCollins Publishers.
All rights reserved. Manufactured in China.
No part of this book may be used or reproduced in any manner whatsoever without
written permission except in the case of brief quotations embodied in critical articles
and reviews. For information address HarperCollins Children's Books, a division of
HarperCollins Publishers, 195 Broadway, New York, NY 10007.
www.harpercollinschildrens.com
Library of Congress catalog card number: 2008922576
ISBN 978-0-06-057390-4 (pbk.)—ISBN 978-0-06-057406-2 (trade bdg.)

15 16 SCP 10 9
First Edition

The Bear family loved their pets and they took very good care of them. They took their dog, Little Lady, for walks every day. They played with their cat, Gracie, with a ball of string or a toy mouse. They kept the bowl of their goldfish, Swish, sparkling clean. Papa had gotten Swish when their first goldfish, Goldie, died. Sadly, goldfish usually don't last very long.

One morning, the whole family went down to the Bear Country Pet Store to do some shopping for their pets. They needed to get some food for Little Lady and some catnip for Gracie. They also needed some new water plants for Swish's bowl.

Brother, Sister, and Honey Bear loved to visit the pet store. Brother liked to watch the puppies. Sister liked to pet the kittens. Honey Bear liked the birds best of all. She liked their bright colors and she liked to talk to them. Sometimes, the birds talked back.

"Tweet!" said Honey Bear
to a cage full of canaries.
"Tweet! Tweet! Tweet!"
sang the canaries.

"Chirp!" said Honey
Bear to a cage full of finches.
"Chirp! Chirp! Chirp!"
chirped the finches.

Honey Bear saw a cage of parakeets. They were all different colors. They were bright yellow and green and orange and blue. Honey Bear liked them very much.

"Bird!" she said, pointing to them.

One of the parakeets—a bright blue one with a twinkle in its eye—cocked its head.

"Bird!" it said, as plain as could be. "Bird! Bird! Bird!"

"Did you hear that?" said Sister. "That bird can talk!"

"It's a parakeet," explained Papa. "Parakeets can imitate sounds they hear, even words."

"That's neat!" said Brother. "Can we get a parakeet?"

"Well," said Mama, "I don't know. We already have three pets."

"Yes," said Brother. "But Swish is a goldfish, and goldfish usually don't last very long."

"True," said Papa.

"Besides," added Sister, "Honey really likes this one. Look—they can already talk to each other."

Honey Bear had her nose pressed up against the bars of the birdcage.

"Keets!" she said, trying to say "parakeets."

"Keets!" the parakeet said back. "Keets! Keets! Keets!"

"'Keats!' That would be a good name for him," Sister said, laughing.

Once they had picked out a name for the parakeet, they couldn't just leave him in the pet store. So Keats the parakeet came home to the tree house with the Bear family.

Keats was easy to take
care of. They fed him
birdseed every day and
gave him water. They
cleaned his cage, and
once a day they let him out
to fly around for exercise.

When they let him out, his favorite place to go was the top of Papa Bear's head. Keats liked to sit up there nibbling at Papa's fur while he read the evening newspaper.

"Hey!" said Papa. "That tickles!"

After he was out for a while, Keats flew back to his cage to get a special treat—a piece of fruit.

"You know," said Papa one evening, looking around at all their pets, "this place is getting to be a regular pet show."

"A pet show," said Mama to herself. "Hmmm!"

Mama was the Chair of the Beartown Festival Committee. The Beartown Festival was a big street fair that was held every year in Beartown Square. The committee was looking for something to do at the festival that would be fun for cubs. A pet show seemed like a pretty good idea.

A few days later, Mama came home from a meeting of the Beartown Festival Committee.

"Well, it's all settled," she told the family.

"What's all settled?" asked Papa.

"The pet show," said Mama. "There's going to be a big pet show at the Beartown Festival this year."

"A pet show!" said Brother and Sister. "Can we enter Little Lady, Gracie, Swish, and Keats?"

"Of course!" said Mama. "That's what pet shows are for."

"Hooray!" yelled Brother and Sister, jumping up and down.

"Ray!" yelled Honey Bear.

"Ray!" imitated Keats. "Ray! Ray! Ray!"

When the day of the big pet
show arrived, Brother, Sister,
and Honey Bear were very busy.
They gave Little Lady and
Gracie baths and brushed their
coats till they shone.

Gracie wore a big pink
ribbon and Little Lady had
a glittery new collar.

Swish's bowl was cleaned and scrubbed. There was a new underwater castle in the bowl, too. It had a drawbridge and a little catapult on top.

Even Keats's birdcage was bright and shiny. Instead of plain newspaper, Sister put the colorful comics section of the paper on the bottom of the cage.

The Bear family and their pets all piled into the car to drive to Beartown Square.

It was quite a scene. There were cubs with their pets from all over Bear Country.

There were a lot of dogs: big dogs and little dogs, shaggy dogs and fancy dogs, barky dogs and shy dogs.

There were a lot of cats: long-haired cats
and scruffy cats, cats with kittens and cats with
mittens, cats who purred and cats who hissed.

There were quite a few bunnies, hamsters, guinea pigs, gerbils, and mice, too.

Keats was not the only bird by a long shot. There were dozens of parakeets and canaries, as well as brightly colored parrots, macaws, and cockatoos.

There were plenty of fish to keep Swish company, along with other water creatures like turtles and frogs.

Some cubs had truly unusual pets. Too Tall Grizzly brought his pet garter snake, Slither. Barry Bruin even had a pet skunk!

"Don't worry," he told everyone. "He's deodorized!"

"That's a relief!" said Mayor Honeypot, who was the judge of the show.

Queenie McBear created quite a stir when she showed up riding her pony. The other cubs were a little jealous. They wished they had ponies, too. But then Queenie let them take turns riding her pony and they forgot all about being jealous.

Mayor Honeypot had a clipboard and he took notes
about all the pets. Brother and Sister looked nervously at
each other. They wondered if their pets had a chance to win
a prize ribbon. Many of the pets at the show seemed very
special compared to their plain old dog, cat, fish, and bird.

The Mayor came to Keats's cage.
"Hello, little bird," said the Mayor.
"What's your name? My name is Mayor Honeypot."

"Honey!" said Keats. "Honey! Honey! Honey!"

The Mayor laughed. "What a clever little bird!" he said, and made a note on his clipboard.

Finally, after he looked at every pet in the show, Mayor Honeypot climbed up on a platform to make an announcement.

"I know you are all waiting to hear which pets will get prize ribbons," he began. "But after much careful thought, I have decided that I can't decide. Since all the pets here are very, very special to the cubs who brought them, I believe that they all should receive a ribbon!"

"YEA!" cried all the cubs.

There were ribbons for the
biggest pet and the smallest pet . . .

for the fanciest cat and the
cutest kitten . . .

for the shaggiest dog and
the scratchiest dog.

Barry Bruin's skunk got ribbon for "Most Unusual et" and Too-Tall Grizzly's nake for "Quietest Pet."

Little Lady got the ribbon for "Best Collar" and Gracie for "Biggest Bow." Swish was "Best Behaved." And Keats was given the ribbon for "Cleverest Bird."

"We always thought Keats was clever," Sister told Mayor Honeypot when he pinned the ribbon on the parakeet's cage. "Now we have a ribbon to prove that he is the cleverest bird in all Bear Country!"

"One small correction," said the Mayor, looking inside the cage. "*She* is the cleverest bird in all Bear Country!"

They looked inside the cage. There, resting on the comics page on the bottom, was a little white egg.

"Where did that come from?" asked Sister.

"I guess Keats must have laid it," said Papa, scratching his head.

"Then Keats . . ." gulped Brother, "is a *girl*!"

"That explains why he . . . I mean *she* . . . is so clever." Sister laughed.

"Very funny," said Brother. "But 'Keats' doesn't sound like a girl's name. Maybe we should change it to 'Keatsie.'"

"How about 'Cutsie'?" suggested Sister.

"Perfect," agreed Brother. "Our clever little parakeet, Cutsie!"

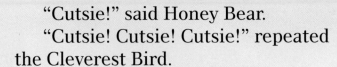

"Cutsie!" said Honey Bear.
"Cutsie! Cutsie! Cutsie!" repeated
the Cleverest Bird.